YASMIN
IN CHARGE

WITHDRAWN

~~San Diego~~
Public Library

3 ~~????~~ 10049 47?7

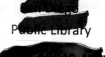

written by
SAADIA FARUQI

illustrated by
HATEM ALY

PICTURE WINDOW BOOKS
a capstone imprint

To Mariam for inspiring me, and Mubashir for helping me find the right words—S.F.

To my sister, Eman, and her amazing girls, Jana and Kenzi—H.A.

Yasmin is published by Picture Window Books,
a Capstone imprint
1710 Roe Crest Drive
North Mankato, Minnesota 56003
www.mycapstone.com

Text © 2019 Saadia Faruqi
Illustrations © 2019 Picture Window Books

All rights reserved. No part of this publication may be reproduced in whole or in part, or stored in a retrieval system, or transmitted in any form or by any means, electronic, mechanical, photocopying, recording, or otherwise, without written permission of the publisher.

Cataloging-in-Publication Data is on file with the Library of Congress.
ISBN: 978-1-5158-4272-9 (paperback)
ISBN: 978-1-5158-4273-6 (eBook PDF)

Summary: In this collection of four stories, Yasmin takes charge of some sticky situations! At home, at school, or out and about, Yasmin faces challenges head on with creativity and quick thinking. Whether she's creating a new recipe, finding a way to rescue a stuck toy for a little friend, or fixing a monkey mishap at the zoo, a clever solution to any problem is right under her nose!

Editor: Kristen Mohn
Designer: Lori Bye

Design Elements:
Shutterstock: Art and Fashion, rangsan paidaen

Printed in Canada.
PA47

TABLE OF CONTENTS

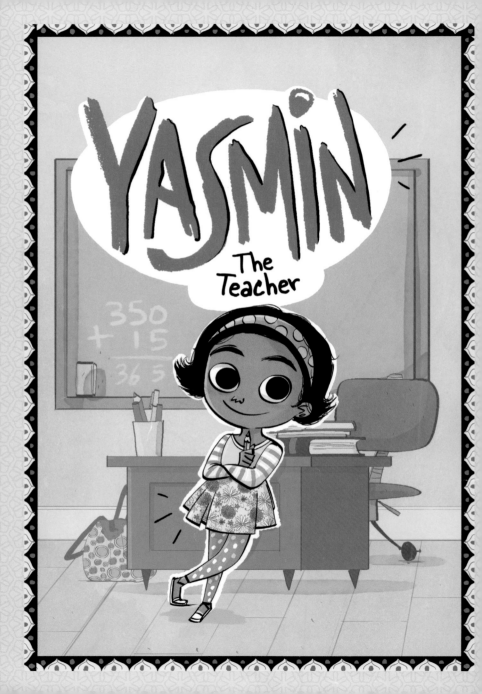

CHAPTER 1

A Present

Yasmin's Aunt Zara came over to Yasmin's house for tea.

"I have a present for you, jaan!" Aunt Zara said. She handed Yasmin a package.

Yasmin ripped it open.

A box of colored pencils!

"I love to color!" Yasmin said.

Then Yasmin noticed a

delicious smell. She held

the pencils up to her nose.

They were scented! Vanilla,

strawberry, mango, chocolate!

"Shukriya! Thank you so

much!" Yasmin cried. "Please

come again with more presents!"

Aunt Zara laughed.

The next day at school, Yasmin
showed her present to Emma and Ali.
"Smell my new pencils," she said.

Ali took a big sniff. "Awesome! I
wish I had some."

Yasmin was about to say that
Emma and Ali could both choose
a pencil to keep. But then the
bell rang.

CHAPTER 2

Yasmin in Charge

In math class Ms. Alex handed out worksheets. "Work quietly, please," she said.

The problems were difficult, but Yasmin could do them. Counting. Addition. Subtraction.

A knock on the door surprised the students. It was Mr. Nguyen, the principal. "Ms. Alex, can I see you for a minute, please?"

Ms. Alex said, "I'm leaving Yasmin in charge. You all must stay as quiet as little mice. And please finish your worksheets!"

She stepped into the hall and closed the door.

Yasmin couldn't believe she was in charge. She wanted to make Ms. Alex proud.

"Hey, everybody!" yelled Ali.

"Watch my cool moves!"

Ali started dancing on the reading
mat. The other students giggled.

Emma began to color on her notepad. "I'm going to draw Yasmin the teacher!" she said loudly.

"Shh!" hissed Yasmin. "We have to be quiet as little mice."

But everyone just talked and laughed. And nobody did their worksheets.

The class was out of control!

CHAPTER 3

The Scented-Pencil Solution

Yasmin felt like crying. What could she do to make Ms. Alex proud?

"Please do your worksheets!" Yasmin said.

Nobody listened.

Emma was almost done with her picture. "I need pink," she said. "Does anyone have pink?"

That gave Yasmin an idea. The scented pencils! She had plenty to share. She got out her box and waved it in the air.

"How about a competition?" she shouted.

Everyone stopped and looked at her.

"I'll give a scented pencil as a prize to whoever completes the worksheet!" she said.

The students were suddenly

quiet as little mice. They sat back

down and worked hard at counting,

addition, and subtraction.

Ali raised his hand. He needed help. Yasmin showed him how to answer the problem.

"I win!" Ali said as he finished the worksheet.

"Good job!" Yasmin said. "Which pencil would you like?"

Ali chose chocolate. "Thanks, Yasmin!"

Next was Emma. "I'll take strawberry," she said. "Thank you, Yasmin!"

Soon all the students had finished and were quietly drawing with their new pencils.

Ms. Alex returned. "Such well-behaved children!" she said. "Yasmin, you've been an excellent teacher today!"

Yasmin grinned. "Thanks, but I'm glad to be a student again!"

CHAPTER 1

Party Prep

On Saturday morning, Yasmin woke up very excited. Tonight they were having a party! Music, friends, and best of all—staying up late! She could hardly wait.

But first there was a lot
of work to be done. Cooking,
cleaning, and more!

After breakfast, Baba began

vacuuming the living room.

"Want to help, Yasmin?" he asked.

"I'll take polish patrol!"

Yasmin said.

Yasmin wiped the coffee table until it shone.

She polished the mirror till it sparkled.

And she washed the windows till they squeaked. Phew!

"Good girl!" Baba hugged
Yasmin. "Let's go see if Mama
needs help."

CHAPTER 2

Too Spicy

The kitchen was busy too.
Yasmin looked at all the food
spread out. Fruits, vegetables,
chicken, rice. And lots of spices!
These were the building blocks of
all the dishes they would cook.

Mama clapped her hands. "Our little helper is here! Taste my fruit chaat, Yasmin."

Yasmin took a bite, then puckered her lips. "Too sour," she said.

Nani was cooking biryani.

"Here, try this," she offered.

Yasmin did, then fanned her mouth. "Too spicy!" she said with a gasp.

Nana laughed. "Here, drink some chai," he suggested.

Yasmin sipped, then spit it out.

"Too hot!" she yelled. Chai dribbled down her chin. "And too messy!"

"There's nothing for me to eat," Yasmin complained. "Why does Pakistani food have to be so spicy or sour or messy?"

Mama frowned. "Yasmin, we should be grateful for the blessings we have."

"Why don't you choose a dish to cook?" Baba said to Yasmin.

She thought. What could she cook that wasn't spicy, wasn't sour, and wasn't messy?

First she tried sandwiches. Too boring.

Then she tried a seven-layer dip. Too many layers!

Maybe a dessert? Too gooey! She threw her spoon on the counter and pouted.

Baba shook his head and sighed.

"Go take a break, Yasmin," he said.

CHAPTER 3

Yasmin's Party Surprise

Yasmin moped in her room. She opened her closet to admire the sparkly shalwar kameez she would wear for the party.

She turned to her jewelry box. Which earrings would match her dress? She held up her favorite pair.

Aha! Yasmin knew what she was going to cook! She ran back down to the kitchen.

"I have an idea!" she shouted.

"I'll help," Nana offered. "You

be the chef, I'll be your helper." He

bowed, and Yasmin giggled.

Before long, it was evening.
Yasmin came downstairs in her
new kameez. The guests were just
beginning to arrive.

Aunties and uncles. Cousins
and friends. "What a lovely dress,
Yasmin!" they all said.

The table was spread with all the food. But there was one more dish to be served.

Nana came out of the kitchen carrying Yasmin's special recipe. It wasn't spicy or sour or messy, and it was easy to eat.

"Chicken, veggie, and fruit kebab!" she announced. "A complete meal on a stick!"

Nani was the oldest, so she tasted the kebab first.

"Delicious!" she cried. "Even better than my biryani."

Nana grinned. "Good work, Chef Yasmin!"

Yasmin took a bite of kebab. "Pretty good, but I think it needs just a pinch of spice," she said.

Everyone laughed.

CHAPTER 1

Field Trip

Yasmin and Mama walked together to school one morning. At least Mama walked. Yasmin skipped. She was very excited. Today her class was taking a field trip to the zoo.

"Here's your lunch, Yasmin," said Mama, handing her a brown bag. "There's fruit in there for a snack too."

Yasmin hugged her mother and boarded the bright yellow bus.

Yasmin looked around. She'd

never been on a school bus before.

Emma waved to her. "Yasmin,

sit with me!"

"Hey, your brown bag is just like mine!" Yasmin said to Emma.

"Mine too!" Ali said, popping up behind them. His bag was big! The girls laughed.

"Ready, class?" asked Ms. Alex.

"Ready!" the students shouted.

The ride to the zoo was very long. The students sang songs and told jokes. Ali's jokes were the funniest.

"What's a kangaroo's favorite game?" he asked. "Hop Scotch!"

CHAPTER 2

Meet the Animals

The zoo was full of all kinds of animals. Ms. Alex led the way. First was a pool for seals.

"Look, they're taking a bath!" Yasmin said.

A seal swam toward them. It splashed them all with water!

"Don't stand too close," Ms. Alex warned. "Remember, this is the animals' home, not yours."

Next they walked to the elephant yard. Yasmin counted three elephants: a mama, a baba, and a baby.

"How adorable!" cried Emma.

The baba elephant walked over and snatched Ali's cap from his head.

"Hey!" shouted Ali. "Give it back!"

Finally, they reached the monkey area. *Bandars!* Yasmin's favorite.

A zookeeper was waiting for them. "Hello, kids," he said. "I'm Dave. It's the monkeys' lunchtime. Would anyone like to help me?"

All the students raised their hands. Yasmin tried to raise hers the highest.

"Please pick me," she whispered.

"How about you, in the purple top?" Dave said. He pointed to Yasmin.

"Yes!" Yasmin cheered.

Dave gave Yasmin a big bowl of fruit. It had slices of apples, bananas, and oranges.

"Fruit salad!" said Emma.

Yasmin carefully walked toward the monkeys. They squealed and chattered with excitement.

But suddenly, Yasmin tripped!

The bowl of fruit went flying . . .

right into the pond.

CHAPTER 3

Hungry Monkeys

The monkeys were upset. They wanted their lunch! They screeched and howled. Yasmin's heart thumped. Would Dave be angry too?

Then she remembered the lunch bag in her backpack.

What had Mama packed?

Yasmin opened it.

A banana!

"Can I share my fruit with the monkeys?" Yasmin asked Dave.

"I guess it would be all right, just this once," Dave said. He broke the banana into pieces for Yasmin.

A baby monkey climbed onto Yasmin's lap. She held very still as the monkey nibbled banana from her hand. It tickled!

Then Emma took out her brown bag. "I have two oranges," she offered.

The other students took out their brown bags too. Soon all the monkeys had fruit to eat.

"Now it's time for *our* lunch!"
Ms. Alex said. "Let's go to the
playground and eat."

Yasmin waved goodbye to the
monkeys.

"Bye, bandars! I'll come again
someday, little friends!"

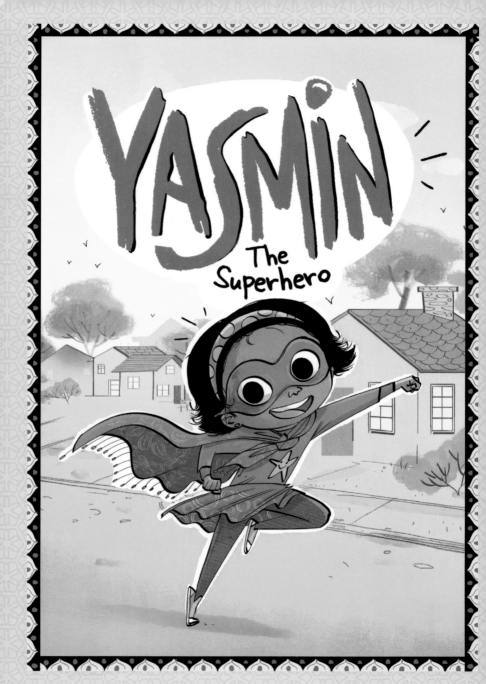

CHAPTER 1

Super Yasmin

Yasmin loved reading with Baba. Her favorite stories were about superheroes.

Baba closed the book.

"I wish I were a superhero," Yasmin said.

"What do you like about
superheroes?" Baba asked.

Yasmin thought. "Well, they
save people," she said.

"From what?" asked Mama.

"From evil villains, of course!"
Yasmin said.

Mama laughed. "Enough
reading," she said. "The weather
is perfect. Why don't you go
outside and play?"

Yasmin skipped to Nana and Nani's room. "I'm Super Yasmin!" she announced. "I'm going outside to defeat evil villains!"

"That sounds important," Nani said. "Every superhero needs a costume."

Nani took her dupatta and draped it over Yasmin's shoulders. "Here is your cape."

Nana brought out his old sleep mask. He cut two holes for her eyes.

"Now you look just like a
superhero," Nana said.

"Thanks!" Yasmin waved.

"I'm off to save the world!"

CHAPTER 2

Who Needs Help?

Yasmin went outside. Lots of children were playing. Some rode bikes. Some kicked a soccer ball.

Yasmin searched everywhere. She didn't see any evil villains. What was the point of being a superhero if there were no villains to defeat?

"Hello, Yasmin!" It was

Emma's mom. She was bringing

in groceries from her car.

Oops! A bag fell and groceries

rolled down the street.

Yasmin ran and caught them all. "Here you go, Mrs. Winters," she said.

"Oh, you saved the day, Yasmin!" Mrs. Winters said. "Thank you so much."

Yasmin continued her search for villains. Maybe one was hiding behind this tree! Nope.

"Hey, Yasmin," Ali called from his front porch. "This math problem is really hard. Can you help me?"

Yasmin figured out the answer in a jiffy. "Four hundred and seventy-five," she told him.

"You're so good at math, Yasmin,"

Ali said. "Thanks a million!"

Yasmin waved and kept walking.

She needed to find a villain.

CHAPTER 3

A Real Hero

At the end of the street, a little girl was crying. Her ball was stuck on a roof. Yasmin looked around. A big stick lay on the ground.

"Don't worry," she told the little girl. "This will do the trick."

The girl was happy to get her ball back. "Thank you! Thank you!" She jumped up and down.

"You're welcome," said Yasmin.

Where were all the villains? she wondered.

Yasmin went back home,

disappointed. Baba was waiting

for her with a glass of cool lassi.

"Super Yasmin is back!"

Baba said.

"I'm not a superhero,"
Yasmin mumbled. "I didn't find
a single evil villain to defeat."

She took a sip of her lassi and
sighed.

Baba hugged her close.

"I saw that you helped many
people on our street today,"
he said. "That's what real
superheroes do!"

"They do?" asked Yasmin.

"Yes! Evil villains are only in story books," Baba said. "In real life, superheroes are the ones who go out of their way to be kind and helpful."

Yasmin gulped down her lassi. "You're right. I did help!" she exclaimed. "I guess I really am Super Yasmin!"

Baba laughed. "Come inside now," he said. "Even superheroes have to do their homework."

Think About It, Talk About It

* It takes courage to be a leader or to try something new. How do you give yourself courage when you need it?

* What are some special recipes that your family makes for parties or holidays? What would you change about them if you could?

* Imagine you are going to a zoo that has every animal in the world. If you could choose only three animals to visit, which would you choose?

* Superheroes have special powers or abilities—and so do people! What do you think Yasmin's super powers are? What are your super powers?

Learn Urdu with Yasmin!

Yasmin's family speaks both English and Urdu. Urdu is a language from Pakistan. Maybe you already know some Urdu words!

baba (BAH-bah)—father

bandar (BAHN-dar)—monkey

dupatta (doo-PAH-tah)—a shawl or scarf

hijab (HEE-jahb)—scarf covering the hair

jaan (jahn)—life; a sweet nickname for a loved one

kameez (kuh-MEEZ)—a long tunic or shirt

lassi (LAH-see)—a yogurt drink

nana (NAH-nah)—grandfather on mother's side

nani (NAH-nee)—grandmother on mother's side

salaam (sah-LAHM)—hello

shalwar (SHAL-wahr)—loose pants

shukriya (shuh-KREE-yuh)—thank you

Pakistan Fun Facts

Yasmin and her family are proud of their Pakistani culture. Yasmin loves to share facts about Pakistan!

Location

Pakistan is on the continent of Asia, with India on one side and Afghanistan on the other.

Islamabad

PAKISTAN

(Salaam means Peace)

Language

The national language of Pakistan is Urdu, but English and several other languages are also spoken there.

Population

Pakistan's population is about 207,774,520, making it the world's sixth-most populous country.

First Female Leader

Benazir Bhutto became the first female Prime Minister of Pakistan, and of any Muslim nation.

Make a Paper Bag Superhero!

SUPPLIES:

- lunch-size paper bag
- construction paper
- scissors
- markers or crayons
- glue stick or tape
- pipe cleaners
- optional: glitter, yarn (for hair), other art supplies

STEPS:

1. Flatten the paper bag and put bottom of bag at top. Draw eyes and a mouth on the folded part of the bag.

2. Cut a mask out of construction paper, or draw one on with marker. Use construction paper to make a cape. Decorate the mask and cape however you like! Glue them onto the paper bag to make the superhero's costume.

3. Glue or tape pipe cleaners to the sides of the bag for the superhero's arms.

4. Create a logo for the front of your superhero. Use your initial or draw a symbol. Use other art supplies to add finishing touches to your superhero, and you're done!

About the Author

Saadia Faruqi is a Pakistani American writer, interfaith activist, and cultural sensitivity trainer previously profiled in *O Magazine*. She is author of the adult short-story collection, *Brick Walls: Tales of Hope & Courage from Pakistan*. Her essays have been published in *Huffington Post*, *Upworthy*, and *NBC Asian America*. She resides in Houston, Texas, with her husband and children.

About the Illustrator

Hatem Aly is an Egyptian-born illustrator whose work has been featured in multiple publications worldwide. He currently lives in beautiful New Brunswick, Canada, with his wife, son, and more pets than people. When he is not dipping cookies in a cup of tea or staring at blank pieces of paper, he is usually drawing books. One of the books he illustrated is *The Inquisitor's Tale* by Adam Gidwitz, which won a Newbery Honor and other awards, despite Hatem's drawings of a farting dragon, a two-headed cat, and stinky cheese.